The Apple Tree Alien

A story in a
familiar setting

First published in 2005 by
Franklin Watts
96 Leonard Street
London
EC2A 4XD

Franklin Watts Australia
45–51 Huntley Street
Alexandria
NSW 2015

A CIP catalogue record for this book is available
from the British Library.

ISBN 0 7496 6125 9 (hbk)
ISBN 0 7496 6131 3 (pbk)

Series Editor: Jackie Hamley
Series Advisors: Dr Barrie Wade, Dr Hilary Minns
Design: Peter Scoulding

Printed in Hong Kong / China

The Apple Tree
Alien

Written by
Penny Dolan

Illustrated by
Roger Fereday

W
FRANKLIN WATTS
LONDON•SYDNEY

Penny Dolan
"I usually write on a computer. But sometimes my bad cat tries to help by walking across the keyboard. Big trouble!"

Roger Fereday
"When I draw I like to look out into my garden. I haven't seen any aliens yet, but I keep looking!"

Harry looked into

Mrs Green's garden. Yikes!

A strange creature was walking down the path.

It wore a strange suit, a strange hat and very strange gloves.

"It's an alien from outer space!" thought Harry.

The creature walked slowly to the end of the garden, where Mrs Green had her apple trees.

Harry ran to tell his dad.

But when Dad looked,
there was no one there.

Next day, Dad forgot his door key.

"Come in my house and wait," smiled Mrs Green.

Suddenly Harry gave a shout.

"It's the alien!" he yelled.

There were the strange hat,
and the strange suit,
and the strange gloves!

"It's not a space suit," laughed
Mrs Green.

"If you can be very quiet,
I'll show you my secret."

At the end of the garden were
three small white houses.

All around was a loud buzzing
sound. "Beehives!" gasped Harry.
Mrs Green nodded.

Mrs Green told Harry all about her bees. First she showed him her beekeeper's clothes.

Next she showed him a
honeycomb in a jar.

Then she asked: "Shall I make
you some toast and honey?"

"Yes please!" said Harry.

It tasted delicious. "Out of this world!" laughed Dad.

Notes for parents and teachers

READING CORNER has been structured to provide maximum support for new readers. The stories may be used by adults for sharing with young children. Primarily, however, the stories are designed for newly independent readers, whether they are reading these books in bed at night, or in the reading corner at school or in the library.

Starting to read alone can be a daunting prospect. READING CORNER helps by providing visual support and repeating words and phrases, while making reading enjoyable. These books will develop confidence in the new reader, and encourage a love of reading that will last a lifetime!

If you are reading this book with a child, here are a few tips:

1. Make reading fun! Choose a time to read when you and the child are relaxed and have time to share the story.

2. Encourage children to reread the story, and to retell the story in their own words, using the illustrations to remind them what has happened.

3. Give praise! Remember that small mistakes need not always be corrected.

READING CORNER covers three grades of early reading ability, with three levels at each grade. Each level has a certain number of words per story, indicated by the number of bars on the spine of the book, to allow you to choose the right book for a young reader:

GRADE 1	GRADE 2	GRADE 3
50 words	130 words	250 words
70 words	160 words	350 words
100 words	200 words	450 words